This book is a gift to

_____

This year they have been...

Naughty ☐   Nice ☐

Santa x

Dedicated to my Grandparents

Thank you for all the fun & laughter over the years.
Loved and missed always, but especially at Christmas.

Printed in the United Kingdom.

First Printing, 2018

ISBN 978-1-9993187-0-3

Blonc Books

Self Published

www.LittleElfRay.com

Little Elf Ray
SAVES THE DAY

WRITTEN BY
ROSS HAMMOND

ILLUSTRATED BY
SEMIH AKGÜL

It was Christmas Eve at the North Pole.

The elves had finished building a brand new, state-of-the-art, magnificent sleigh.

Santa was so pleased, he decided to take a test flight with some of his reindeer.

Ray, the littlest of all the elves, went along with him...

Santa was looking around his sleigh, when he accidently pulled on the reins a little too hard.

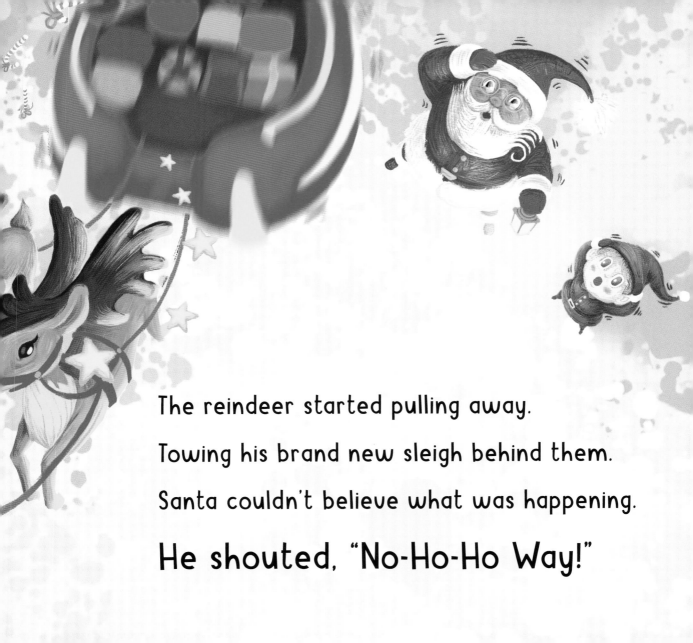

The reindeer started pulling away.

Towing his brand new sleigh behind them.

Santa couldn't believe what was happening.

He shouted, "No-Ho-Ho Way!"

What was he going to do?

He stroked his beard to help him to gather his thoughts until he came up with a plan.

He shouted to Elf Ray, "Go get Rudolph!"

... Ray ran around in circles...

Off ran Little Elf Ray...

... while trying to find his way back to Santa's Grotto.

... unfortunately, in his panic...

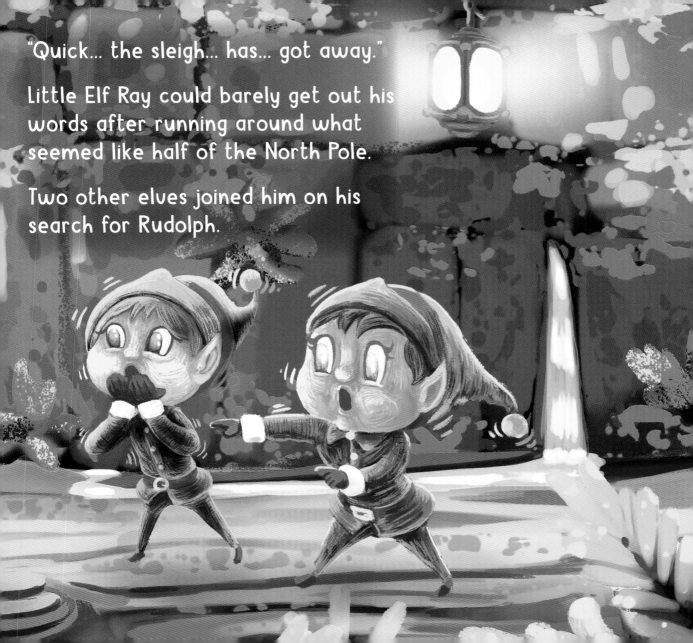

"Quick... the sleigh... has... got away."

Little Elf Ray could barely get out his words after running around what seemed like half of the North Pole.

Two other elves joined him on his search for Rudolph.

Ray hopped onto Rudolph's back.

He pointed to the faint trail of magic sparkles left by the fast sleigh and shouted, "Follow that sleigh!".

Rudolph's nose lit up the way as they took off into the air.

Ray was holding on with all his strength as Rudolph galloped through the sky.

As they neared the sleigh,
Ray knew what he had to do.

He stood on Rudolph's back,
not daring to look down, his
little knees shaking with fear.

He took a deep
breath and jumped.

THUD... Ray landed in the sleigh,
his face slamming onto the
wooden floor.

His heart was pounding very fast!

He straightened up, his nose was
even redder than Rudolph's.

He grabbed the reins and shouted as loudly as he could, **"TAKE US HOME!"**

The sleigh touched down and began to slide along the snow, finally coming to a stop next to Santa and the elves.

Everyone cheered! "Hooray for Ray! Hooray for Ray!"

And that is how Christmas was saved,
all by a brave little elf called Ray!

Can you find...?

Squish The Squirrel and the Christmas items below have gone missing in this book!

Can you find them all?

Ross Hammond - Author

"I created this book to show children that even though they are little they can achieve great things. Merry Christmas"

Semih Akgül - Illustrator

"Ever since I was a child it was my dream to illustrate a children's book. My dream has now come true!"